Wilma J the Worry Machine

published by

National Center for Youth Issues

Practical Guidance Resources
Educators Can Trust

ncyi.org

www.ncyi.org

For Natalie
–Julia

Duplication and Copyright

National Center for Youth Issues
Practical Guidance Resources
Educators Can Trust
ncyi.org

P.O. Box 22185
Chattanooga, TN 37422-2185
423.899.5714 • 800.477.8277
fax: 423.899.4547
www.ncyi.org

ISBN: 978-1-937870-01-0
© 2012 National Center for Youth Issues, Chattanooga, TN
All rights reserved.

Written by: Julia Cook
Illustrations by: Anita DuFalla
Design by: Phillip W. Rodgers
Published by National Center for Youth Issues
Softcover

Printed by RR Donnelley • Reynosa, Mexico • November 2012

My name is Wilma Jean. Last Friday, I didn't want to get out of bed because I didn't want to go to school…so I pretended to be asleep.

I think I had the worry flu.

Every morning, when I wake up, I feel just fine, but then…

My tongue gets salty,
my throat gets tight,
I grit my teeth
'cause nothin' feels right.

My stomach feels like
it's tied up in a knot.
My knees lock up, and
my face feels hot.

Worry, Worry, Worry!

You know what I mean?
I'm Wilma Jean,
The Worry Machine.

On Friday, I was worried about spelling, because we had a spelling test.

"**What if**
I forget how to spell?

What if
everyone finishes before me?"

I worried about math.

"**What if** I get picked to do a problem up on the board in front of everyone?

What if the kids make fun of my hair again?

What if I get the problem wrong?

What if they write about it in the school newspaper?"

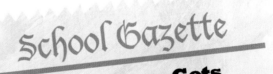

School Gazette

Wilma Jean Gets Math Problem Wrong AGAIN

I worried about school lunch.

" **What if**

we have buttered carrots, and the lunch ladies make me eat them?
I can't stand buttered carrots!"

"Get up Wilma Jean," my mom said. "It's time to get ready for school. I know you're not asleep because you're making that pickle face...the one you make when you're worried about something. If you don't stop worrying so much, you're going to make yourself sick again."

"*Too late*." I thought to myself.

By the time I got to school, I felt like I had swallowed an elephant playing the banjo.

Luckily, I didn't forget how to spell, I didn't get picked in math, and for lunch we had buttered corn. I **LOVE** buttered corn!

Then, I started to think about my afternoon. "What if Aberdeen has another orthodontist appointment after lunch…Who will I play with at recess?"

"**What if** I get picked last for a team in P.E.?

What if they write about that in the school newspaper?"

"What if

I'm so busy getting all of my homework together after school, that I miss the bus, and I have to walk home, and it's snowing, and I don't have my boots?

What if

my after school snack is tapioca pudding?

I can't stand tapioca pudding!"

"'Wilma Jean, honey,' the lunch lady said, 'finish your corn!

You're going to miss recess!

And what's wrong with your face?

You look like you just bit down on a sour pickle!'"

When I walked out onto the playground, I saw Aberdeen right away. Her orthodontist appointment was after school.

In P.E., Reggie Beck got chosen to be a team captain, and he's had a crush on me for years, so he picked me first!

I made it to the bus after school in plenty of time, and when I got home, my mom gave me butterscotch pudding for my snack.

I **LOVE** butterscotch pudding!

I looked across the room and as soon as I saw Aberdeen's birthday present on the counter,

Aberdeen

My tongue got salty. My throat got tight.
I gritted my teeth, 'cause nothin' felt right.

My stomach felt like it was tied up in a knot.
My knees locked up, and my face got hot!

"Wilma Jean…, you're making the pickle face again. What are you worried about now?" my mom asked.

"I can't go to Aberdeen's birthday skating party tomorrow afternoon!" I said.

"Why? You love skating and you love Aberdeen."

"Because, what if I get there late and everybody is already skating and they run out of skates?

What if I forget how to skate and I wipe out and everybody laughs at me?

What if they write about that in the town newspaper?

What if Aberdeen is so busy with all of her other friends that she doesn't have time to skate with me and I have to skate all by myself?

What if.."

15

"What if? What if? What if? Wilma Jean!

If you don't stop worrying so much, you're going to make yourself sick again.

Now I'm starting to really worry about you!"

My mom made the pickle face just like me. Then, she picked up the phone and called my doctor, my principal, my school counselor, my teacher, my accordion instructor, the mayor of our town, and the governor of our state (not really the last two.)

When she finally hung up the phone, her pickle face went away.

DOCTOR OFFICE

The next day, my mom made sure that I was the first one at Aberdeen's birthday party, so I had my choice of skates. I only wiped out once, and I don't think anyone noticed. And, everyone at the party talked to me and we all skated together, so I never felt left out. I had the best time ever!

The rest of my weekend was great and I didn't have to make the pickle face once.

But on Monday morning, my pickle face came back.

"Don't worry Wilma Jean, my mom said.
From now on, things are going to be different."

My mom drove me to school early so we could
have a special meeting with my teacher.

"Wilma Jean, you seem to worry a lot," my teacher said. "Everybody worries about things, and worrying a little bit is a good thing most of the time, but when you worry so much that it keeps you from doing the things that you want to do, we need to figure out a way to help you."

"I want you to tell me everything you are worried about at school. I'm going to write each worry you have down on a note card."

"Well," I said...

"I always worry when we take a test.

I'm just afraid that I won't do my best.

I'm always scared that I'll run out of time, even though you say,

'Oh, you'll be just fine!'"

"I worry about doing my math on the board.

I might get it wrong and get a bad score.

Then all of the kids won't think that I'm smart.

And, I won't get a smiley on the Smiley Math Chart."

"I worry about lunch and what they will serve. If they serve buttered carrots, I know I will hurl.

I worry that kids will make fun of my hair. I try to fix it, but it goes everywhere!"

"I worry about having friends
to play with outside.

Last time the girls left me,
and that made me cry.

I worry about missing the bus
at the end of the day.

I worry about naughty kids
and the things that they say."

"I worry about worrying so much,
because that's all I do.

I worry that I'll always have
the bad worry flu.

Oh, and I worry about the weather, too!"

My teacher wrote and wrote and wrote. Then she drew a big line across the board. On the top of the line she wrote the words: "Worries I can control." On the bottom she wrote: "Worries I cannot control." Then she had me stick all of my worries up on the board where I thought they belonged:

"Wilma Jean, I know just what to do.
 I can help you get rid of your bad worry flu.
The things that you worry about are easy to fix.
Just let me use some of my great teacher tricks."

On the chalkboard:

Worries I Can Control

Tests

Math

Worries I Can't Control

Weather

Recess

Lunch

Buses

"When we take tests, I will be sure to give you a little bit of extra time if you need it.

If you are going to be picked for a math problem at the board, I will give you your problem the night before so that you can practice doing it at home."

"I will make sure that you have the lunch menu each week, so that you can bring a sack lunch on buttered carrot days.

My sister is a hair stylist, and she is coming to our class this Thursday for career day to teach everyone how to make their hair look better."

"We can set up some fun recess group games and contests, and even do a lunch bunch so that playing outside with others will be easier for you.

I can help you stay organized throughout the day so that when the bell rings, you have plenty of time to catch the bus."

"I can help you learn to control all of these worries... except the weather.

Nobody can control the weather. For that one we need the worry hat.

Put the worry hat on and think all of your worries that you cannot control into the hat. Turn the hat upside down, and it will hold your worries for you. Then, if you ever want, or need them back, you can put on the hat and 'think' them back into your head."

I let my teacher try out all of her tricks. Believe it or not, I was easy to fix.
She taught me how to be more in control. I feel a lot better 'cause now I just know
what to do with my worries when they're inside my head.
Now, I'll never let worrying keep me in bed!

From now on when I worry, I'll know just what to do
to keep from getting the bad worry flu.

And hopefully,
I won't have to
make the pickle
face as much!

A Note to Parents and Educators:

Anxiety is a subjective sense of worry, apprehension, and/or fear. It is considered to be the number one health problem in America. Although everyone feels anxious from time to time, approximately 10 percent of children have excessive fears and worries that can keep them from enjoying life.* Although quite common, anxiety disorders in children are often misdiagnosed or overlooked. It is normal for everyone to feel fear, worry and apprehension from time to time, but when these feelings prevent a person from doing what he/she wants and/or needs to do, anxiety becomes a disability.

Here are a few tips for dealing with an anxious child:
- Genuinely accept your child's concerns.
- Listen to your child's perceptions and gently correct misinformation.
- Patiently encourage your child to approach a feared situation one step at a time until it becomes familiar and manageable.
- Always try to get your child to events on time, or early – being late can elevate levels of anxiety.
- Continually set equal expectations for all kids anxious or not. Expecting a child to be anxious will only encourage anxiety.
- Role-play strategies – how to react in certain situations. – Explore both best case scenarios and worst case scenarios using realistic evidence.
- Build your child's personal strengths.
- Help your child organize their school materials for the next day the night before.
- Allow and encourage your child to do things on his own.
- Allow extra time on tests and/or allow students to take tests away from the other students.
- If a child is going to be singled out for a classroom activity, let that child know a day in advance so that he can feel more prepared.
- Designate a "safe person" at school that understands your child's worries and concerns.
- Try not to pass your own fears onto your child.
- Work together as a team (family members, teachers, child, day-care providers etc.)
- Set consequences – don't confuse anxiety with other types of inappropriate behavior. Set limits and consequences so that you don't allow anxiety to enable your child.
- Have reasonable expectations.

* *Helping Your Anxious Child 2nd edition*, Rapee et. al Newharbinger Publications 2008